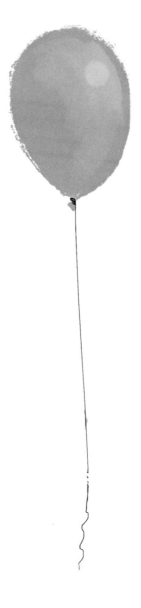

Gabriel Alborozo

The Colour
Thief

BLOOMSBURY

LONDON   NEW DELHI   NEW YORK   SYDNEY

Zot's world had no colour. At all. Anywhere.
No green grass or blue sky, no yellow sun or red flowers.
It made everyone sad.

From his lonely mountain-top, Zot gazed longingly at the distant planet in the night sky. It sparkled with brilliant colour.

Zot thought it must be a very happy place. He decided to go there and find happiness for himself.

Zot's journey to the colourful planet was a long one.
When he arrived, he was amazed by everything he saw.
There was just so much colour!

Everywhere!

Perhaps he could stay here
for ever, and be happy.
But then he thought about all his friends.

He had an idea.
He would take the colour back to his planet . . .

Zot opened his mouth and called out in a strange language.
In reply, all the red soared through the air and into his open bag.

Zot walked to a hill-top.
He looked at the blue sky and the deep blue sea.

Again, he called, and the blue rushed into his bag.

Next Zot stole the green.

The leaves were now grey,
and the grass was almost black.

Zot stole all the colours . . .

calling them to him . . .

until every last colour . . .

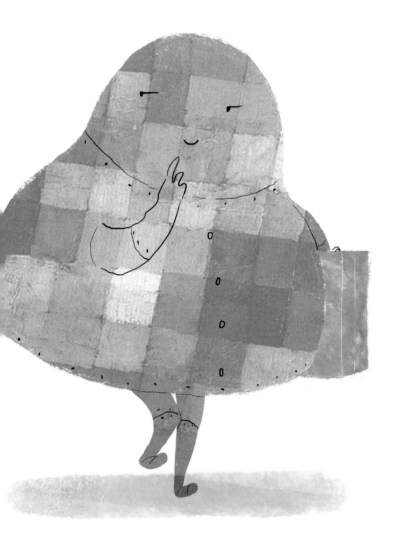

had disappeared.

Apart from one . . .

A boy came bouncing
along with a balloon.
An orange balloon.

Zot wanted that colour too . . .

. . . and he took it.

Then he climbed into his spacecraft and took off.
But when he looked down at the grey planet,
and the boy who looked so sad, Zot knew he must go back.

Carefully, gently, he returned all
the beautiful colours to the boy's world.

The boy watched Zot climb sadly into his ship.
He held out his orange balloon.

Zot grasped it tightly to his chest.
At last, he was truly happy.

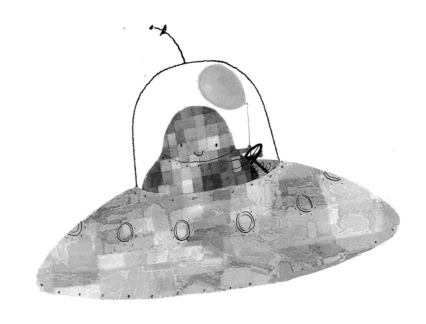

He turned his ship for home.

Zot's friends greeted him,
and the warm glow from the boy's balloon
lit them up and they were happy.

A little colour can go a long, long way.

For Katia Mou ~ GA

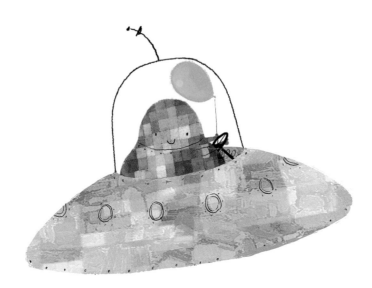

Bloomsbury Publishing, London, New Delhi, New York and Sydney

First published in Great Britain in 2014 by Bloomsbury Publishing Plc
50 Bedford Square, London, WC1B 3DP

This paperback edition first published in 2015

A CIP catalogue record for this book is available from the British Library

ISBN 978 1 4088 4753 4 (HB)
ISBN 978 1 4088 4760 2 (PB)
ISBN 978 1 4088 4761 9 (eBook)

Printed in China by Leo Paper Products, Heshan, Guangdong

1 3 5 7 9 10 8 6 4 2

All papers used by Bloomsbury Publishing are natural, recyclable products made from
wood grown in well-managed forests. The manufacturing processes conform
to the environmental regulations of the country of origin

www.bloomsbury.com

BLOOMSBURY is a registered trademark of Bloomsbury Publishing Plc